"Are you two the only fairies here?" asked Lady Courtney. "I think you're in luck."

Sylva and Poppy flew over to the crate. It had a latch on the front and opened quite easily. Inside was not a jumble of old rubbish that no one would want. Inside was something so marvelous that Sylva and Poppy could hardly believe it.

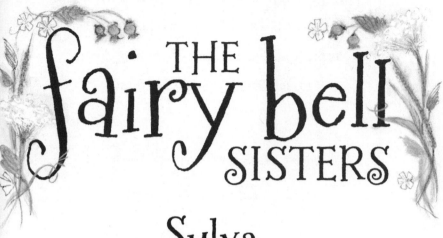

THE fairy bell SISTERS

Sylva
and the
Lost Treasure

Margaret McNamara

ILLUSTRATIONS BY CATHARINE COLLINGRIDGE

BALZER + BRAY
An Imprint of HarperCollins*Publishers*

In the spirit of J. M. Barrie, who created Peter Pan and Tinker Bell, the author has donated a portion of the proceeds from the sale of this book to the Great Ormond Street Hospital.

Balzer + Bray is an imprint of HarperCollins Publishers.

Sylva and the Lost Treasure
Text copyright © 2014 by Margaret McNamara
Illustrations copyright © 2014 by Catharine Collingridge
Map copyright © by Julia Denos
All rights reserved. Printed in the United States of America.

Library of Congress Cataloging-in-Publication Data
McNamara, Margaret.
  Sylva and the lost treasure / Margaret McNamara ; illustrations by Catharine Collingridge. — First edition.
     pages cm. — (The Fairy Bell sisters ; 5)
  Summary: Fairies Sylva Bell and Poppy Flower are overjoyed when they find Queen Mab's old dollhouse, but as the two friends play with it, they start to unlock its secrets and discover its special magic—a magic that has a history of putting friendships to the test.
  ISBN 978-0-06-226721-4 (hardback) — ISBN 978-0-06-226720-7 (paperback)
  [1. Fairies—Fiction. 2. Magic—Fiction. 3. Friendship—Fiction.] I. Collingridge, Catharine, illustrator. II. Title.
PZ7.M47879343Syp 2014   2013047773
[Fic]—dc23   CIP
                                                                                 AC

Typography by Erin Fitzsimmons
14 15 16 17 18 CG/RRDH 10 9 8 7 6 5 4 3 2 1
❖
First Edition

for
Linda, Jane,
and Carol

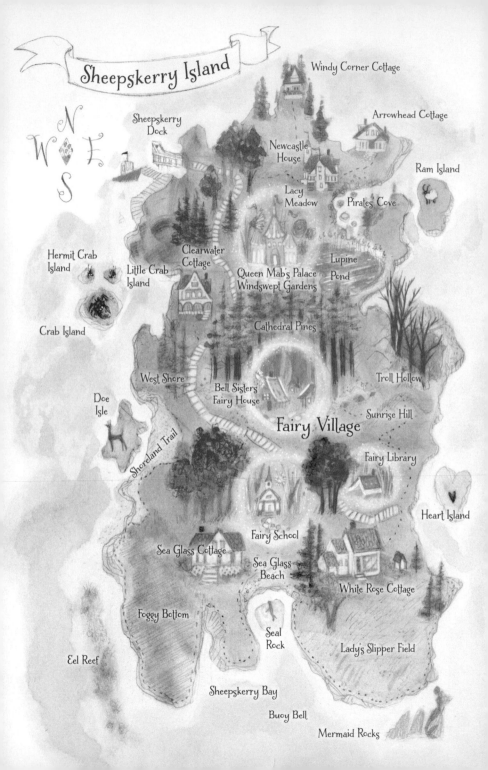

THE
fairy bell
SISTERS

one

In Fairyland, from the far outer isles to the mainland to Sheepskerry Island, where the Fairy Bell sisters live, springtime means spring-cleaning. As the hummingbirds play and the apple blossoms cover the ground with snowy flowers, fairies everywhere clean out their dresser drawers and beat their rugs and take down curtains for their twice-a-year wash.

At the Fairy Bell household, the long week of spring-cleaning was nearly done.

"Has anyone seen Sylva?" Clara called to her

fairy sisters. She was ironing their best linen napkins, the ones with lace on the edges.

"I think she went up to Queen Mab's again—to the petting zoo," said Rosy. She and baby Squeak were scrubbing the breadboard. Or Rosy was scrubbing the breadboard. Squeak was having fun with flour.

"Squeak!" said Squeak.

"That zoo could use a spring-cleaning," said Goldie as she plumped a pillow. "Animals can get awfully stinky."

"I'm not at the petting zoo and animals don't get stinky if you take care of them," Sylva called from her room. "Plus, I did all the zoo cleaning yesterday." She was proud of the way she took care of Queen Mab's animals. "Queen Mab says I'm a natural."

"You may be a natural at cleaning animals' rooms, but what about your own? Have you cleaned under your bed yet?"

"I'm just doing it now!" Sylva said. She peeked under the bed. "Oops," she said. "What a disaster." Sylva didn't want to spend a lot of time sorting through the muddle of shoe bags and clothes and books and shells and twigs and paints that she stored behind her bed ruffle, so with a mighty *push* she shoved them toward the wall, swabbed the mop around quickly, and decided she was finished.

She flew to the top of the stairs. "Can I please go out now, Clara?" she asked. "Poppy promised she'd be ready to go to the jumble pile the minute I put down my mop."

The jumble pile was the best part of spring-cleaning. All the Sheepskerry fairies brought their unwanted items to Queen Mab's palace and left them on her bright green lawn. What a treasure trove it was! Goldie found an antique kimono in the jumble pile one year, which Queen Mab said had come from an island terribly far

away. Rosy claimed a funny little bouncer seat
for Squeakie only last spring, and for weeks on
end, Squeak had bounced up and down every
morning while Rosy warmed her bottle.

Sylva had yet to find anything really worth
calling a treasure in the jumble pile. She'd picked

up some dented thimbles and a couple of water-logged books, but she'd never had a real find.

"If you don't say I'm finished with my chores, I'm going to burst!" said Sylva. "We've got to get up there before the other fairies take the good stuff. I bet those Seaside sisters have already taken everything I would have liked."

"You're done, Sylva," said Clara. "In fact, I think we're all done. Good job. You can go up there whenever you—"

And before Clara could finish her sentence, Sylva was out the door.

"I'll find treasure for all my sisters," she said. "And something very special just for me!"

two

I trust you already know about the Fairy Bell sisters. If you have not met them yet, or even if you have, I'll present them to you now. Here are:

Clara Bell

Rosy Bell

Golden Bell

Sylva Bell

and baby
Squeak

They are Tinker Bell's little sisters—yes, *that* Tinker Bell—and they live in a fairy house on Sheepskerry Island, which is, in fact, not far from where you are reading this right now. There's a map of the island at the front of this book, but you won't find it in any atlases used by grown-ups. Magic islands don't show up on ordinary maps.

The Fairy Bell sisters loved one another very much and got along together without fighting— at least most of the time. And though Sylva loved all her sisters dearly (even Goldie), there was one fairy in all the world she considered her very best friend. And that was Poppy Flower.

Poppy and Sylva were almost exactly the same age. They had known each other since they first popped into the world. They liked all the same things and dressed the same way and sat next to each other at school and played with each other whenever they could. They were even heroes together on the night of the Fairy Ball last summer (even if Sylva was a little bit more of a hero than Poppy).

Two better friends you would never meet. You might even have a best friend, just as Sylva does, and I'm sure you love your friend very much indeed. Maybe you have always been kind and good to your best friend and you two have never exchanged a harsh word. Maybe everything has always been smooth sailing with your best friend and you've never had a stormy moment. Maybe you and your best friend are in complete harmony. And maybe you won't want to read this book.

But if you love your best friend dearly, and want to do everything together, but sometimes—just sometimes—you get a tiny bit cross, and say something you don't quite mean, and drive your friend away, only to find you can't really live without each other . . . then you're very much like Sylva. So turn the page quickly, dear reader. Turn the page and read on.

three

How glad I am that you turned the page!

four

Sylva flew over to the Flower sisters' fairy house.

"Poppy!" she called. "Poppy, I'm all done! Let's go!"

"Nearly finished," Poppy said brightly. She had a kerchief tied over her hair and dust smudges on the tip of her nose. "I just have to sweep the floorboards in the attic and wash my face and I'll be done, too."

Sylva was just about to suggest that she meet Poppy up at the jumble pile when Poppy flew back up to the attic. "Don't leave without me!" Poppy said.

Sylva didn't really want to help with any more chores, but she knew things would go faster with two fairies working together. "I'll do the sweeping," she said with a sigh, "and you wash up. That way, we won't waste any time."

Poppy went off to wash her face and hands, and Sylva made a very quick dash around the attic with a broom. The dust was thick on the floorboards and made a cloud around Sylva as she furiously swept. "Why didn't Poppy do this already?" she grumbled. She made her way from one end of the attic to the other, kicking up dust as she went.

"All set," called Poppy as she came back up the attic stairs. She could hardly see for the clouds of dust. "Sylva?" she called between coughs. "Whatever are you doing?"

"I'm sweeping!" said Sylva, coughing too.

"Not like that!" Poppy said, laughing. "You

have to dampen dust before you sweep it." She went over to a small bucket of water in the corner of the attic. "I'll do it, Sylva. It won't take a minute."

Sylva knew that Poppy's laugh was not meant to be unkind, but still, it hurt a little bit. Sylva had just been trying to help! And how was she supposed to know that Poppy used water to help her sweep?

"There, all done," said Poppy.

"Let's go!" said Sylva.

"Hang on just one more minute while we wash the dust off our faces. We can't show up at Queen Mab's palace like this."

Sylva splashed some springwater on her face as Poppy carefully used a facecloth to get all the smudges off. "Come on, Poppy. We'll miss everything."

"There's tons of stuff in the jumble pile, Sylva. We won't miss a thing."

five

"Faster, Poppy!" said Sylva.

Lacey Cobweb flew up as they approached. "Are you going to the jumble pile? You've missed almost everything!" she said. "The Bakewell sisters took some cookie trays— the ones that weren't bashed up. And the Seaside sisters took a collection of sea glass that Avery had brought up from the schoolhouse attic. It's a lucky thing there were no blues, or Goldie would have grabbed them out of their hands!"

"Did someone mention my name?" asked Goldie. "And, by the way, notice anything different about me?" Goldie swept down from the other side of the jumble pile, wearing a hat the size of a small tabletop.

"Your shoelace is untied?" asked Sylva.

"No, my hat is fabulous!" said Goldie. "You two should hurry. Lady Courtney is getting rid of some stuff from the basement of the palace. But I think most of the best things are gone."

Sylva couldn't bear the thought that she might have missed out on treasures again. All because of Poppy.

"Come on, Poppy, we have to get over there before it's all taken."

Sylva and Poppy flew to the back of the

palace. As short a trip as it was, it still gave them enough time to see lots of other fairies with their hands full of great finds.

"Can you believe Queen Mab doesn't want these beads?" asked Fern Stitch. "I'll sew them onto a bag I'm making for Stemmy's birthday. Don't tell her."

Sylva sped up her flight.

"Look at what I found!" cried Shellie Seaside. "Driftwood in the shape of a baby whale."

There'll be nothing left for me! Sylva thought.

By the time Sylva and Poppy arrived at the lawn of Queen Mab's palace, the jumble pile was not much of a pile at all. It was just a bunch of odds and ends spread out like rubbish on the lawn. Tears pricked Sylva's eyes. She had missed out again.

Of course there were a few things that looked nice—a pretty blue button that would have been prettier if it hadn't been broken in two; a teacup with a crack right down the middle; a baby's chair with three legs . . . and no seat.

Sylva almost said something about how they could have gotten there earlier if Poppy hadn't insisted on dampening the dust, but she thought Poppy might already be feeling bad, and she didn't want to make her feel worse.

Sylva was just about to head sadly back to the Bell fairy house with her one broken button and the cracked teacup when they caught sight of Queen Mab's attendant. Lady Courtney was flying slowly out of the palace, with something very large in her arms.

"Heigh-ho, here's Lady Courtney," said Sylva.

"She'll probably tell us we're not allowed to touch anything," said Poppy.

"Or that we need to curtsy before we approach the jumble pile." They both giggled. "I

think she needs help," said Sylva. "That's a huge crate she's carrying."

The two fairies flew over to Lady Courtney, who was indeed struggling under the weight of a large crate, which looked very old.

"Sylva, Poppy, good afternoon to you," said Lady Courtney.

"May we help you, Lady Courtney?" asked

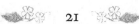

Sylva, using her best manners. "That looks awfully heavy."

"It is heavy," said Lady Courtney. She set the box down with a rattling thump. "Whew! These wings aren't getting any younger."

"Probably a whole box of broken plates and cups," whispered Sylva.

"Plus some dirty old pieces of string," Poppy whispered back. She and Sylva giggled again.

"Are you two the only fairies here?" asked Lady Courtney. "I think you're in luck."

Sylva and Poppy flew over to the crate. It had a latch on the front and opened quite easily. Inside was not a jumble of old rubbish that no one would want. Inside was something so marvelous that Sylva and Poppy could hardly believe it.

Six

"A fairy dollhouse!"

Sylva and Poppy slowly, carefully lifted the dollhouse out of its crate. There was not a scratch or a dent on it. It was in perfect condition.

"It must be very old," said Poppy in a whisper.

"Oh look, it's got everything!" said Sylva. "What a sweet couch in the sitting room." She ran her finger across the dark-red fabric. "It's velvet!"

"Look at the curtains in the bedroom," said Poppy. "Lace!"

"Ooh! The kitchen has tiny little pots and pans hanging on the wall. I think they're real copper!" She looked around some more.

Sylva had always wanted a fairy dollhouse of her own. The one at the Bell sisters' fairy house was Tink's first. Then it got passed down to Clara, then to Rosy, and then to Goldie. By the time it got to Sylva a couple of years ago, it was pretty much destroyed.

But this one—

"It has an attic!" cried Poppy. "With hardly any dust." She gave Sylva a playful nudge. Sylva nudged her back.

Lady Courtney bestowed a rare smile on them both. "Maybe it was magic that brought you here at the exact right moment," she said. "What a treasure you have found. It's yours now, my dears. The queen will be happy it's going to two such good friends." Lady Courtney sighed. "It once belonged to two other young fairies. They too were best friends—a lot like you."

"I thought it was Queen Mab's," said Sylva.

"It was Queen Mab's and—" Lady Courtney started to say something, but then she stopped herself. "Take good care of it, please," was all she told them.

"Of course we will, Lady Courtney!" said Sylva. "Come on, Poppy. Let's fly it home to my house before anyone else sees it. It's ours fair and square."

"Fair and square to share!" said Poppy.

The two friends closed the dollhouse doors and carefully placed the house back in the crate. With some effort, they lifted it together. "I think I'll be able to get it off the ground, Sylva," said Poppy.

"Great! Let's pump our wings and get this home!" said Sylva. They turned in the direction of the Fairy Village.

A sudden rustling of wings stopped them in their tracks. Then they heard an urgent voice.

"Sylva! Poppy! One moment, please!"

seven

Queen Mab!

Poppy and Sylva stopped so suddenly they almost dropped their precious treasure. They tried to curtsy while

they held the huge box between them, but it was pretty much impossible.

They gently set the dollhouse down, which gave them both a moment to think of what to say to Queen Mab.

"It was in the jumble pile!"

"Lady Courtney said—"

"And so we thought—"

Queen Mab smiled. "I didn't mean to startle you, my fairies," she said. "And you're right. I am giving the dollhouse away. I just wanted to make sure it was going to a good home. And I can see it is."

"We're going to share it," said Sylva.

"Of course, Sylva dear. I know that. I suppose I'm just having a little pang about it. Silly of me, really."

Sylva and Poppy did not understand exactly what Queen Mab meant by a pang. Her face had a faraway look. She seemed to be thinking of something that happened a long time ago.

"I'm sure Lady Courtney told you that the dollhouse once belonged to best friends who were a lot like you." Sylva and Poppy nodded. "It was shared by two young fairies who loved each other very much and did everything together."

"One was you . . . ," said Sylva, when the queen was silent for a while.

"Yes, I was one," said Queen Mab, "and the other was my best friend, Nia." She said the name in a whisper.

"We lived here at my palace when we were both young," said Queen Mab. "We thought we would be best friends forever." She stopped talking and wrapped her wings around herself. "But we haven't seen each other in years."

"What happened?" Poppy asked.

Queen Mab shook her head as if she were waking up from a dream.

"Sylva Allegra Bell, you always make me

act in unexpected ways," said the queen. "That story is something that happened long ago. What's happening now is that you two deserve this lovely fairy dollhouse yourselves. Take good care of it, and may it bring you both much joy." And away she flew.

"That's such a sad story about Queen Mab and her friend," said Sylva.

"That would never happen to us," said Poppy.

But neither Poppy nor Sylva could guess that their own friendship would soon be put to a very great test!

eight

"Let's take the dollhouse home," said Sylva. "My sisters will be so jealous!"

"Good idea," said Poppy. "We'll keep it at your fairy house for a while, and then we can move it to mine."

"Well, we *could* take it to your fairy house, eventually," said Sylva. "But I think it's important to have it at our house so that if Tinker Bell comes home, she could see it. Don't you think so, too, Poppy?"

"Yes, yes, I do."

Sylva guessed that Poppy might have wanted

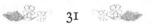

to show off the dollhouse to her own sisters, so she gave that idea some thought. "I'll tell you what," said Sylva. "We'll keep it at my house for part of the time, and then we'll bring it to your house. And just to be completely fair, you can be in charge of the upstairs part of the house"—she knew this would please Poppy, because the upstairs had bedrooms with flowered wallpaper—"and I will be in charge of the downstairs of the house." Sylva actually liked the downstairs better—there was a sweet little piano that she hoped she could make work one day. "Whatever is upstairs belongs to you; whatever is downstairs belongs to me."

"Perfect!" said Poppy. "Good idea!"

It wasn't easy flying with a big crate, but Poppy and Sylva were so good at working together that they did very well, and were back at the Fairy Bell sisters' house in no time.

Clara was at home, having spring-cleaning lemonade with Iris Flower.

"Oh, Clara! Iris! Look what we got from the jumble pile!" Sylva called.

Poppy and Sylva carefully lifted the dollhouse out of the crate. "We're getting good at this," Sylva said with a grin. Iris and Clara were amazed.

"Are you absolutely positive Queen Mab is giving this away?"

"We're positive! She said so herself!" said Sylva.

"She gave it to the two of us," said Poppy. "And we've worked out exactly how we're going to share." Poppy grinned at Sylva, and Sylva grinned back.

With their spring-cleaning all finished, the blessing of Queen Mab on their heads, and the

scent of a hundred daffodils in the air, the two
best friends played with their fairy dollhouse in
the fairy house garden, and didn't even stop for
lunch.

nine

"**S**ylva! Look what I found!"

Sylva was busy arranging the copper pots in the kitchen of her downstairs fairy house. "Just a minute, Poppy," she said. "I need to fix this handle. I wish Tink were here right now. Mending pots and pans is her specialty."

"Ooh, Sylva! It is *so cute!*" Poppy cried. She was at the back of the dollhouse, looking very closely at something on the windowsill of her upstairs rooms.

Sylva came around and looked with her.

"What is it? I don't see anything."

"It's a kitten, Sylva," said Poppy. She pointed to the tiny lump of gray fur on the windowsill of the fairy house attic. "A teeny tiny kitten."

"Ooh! A doll kitten! She's so pretty!" said Sylva, carefully petting the kitten with her pinky finger. "I wish it were a real kitten," she said. "Wouldn't you like to have a pet of your very own?"

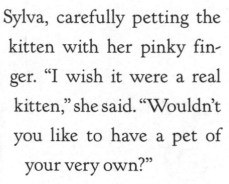

"More than anything!" said Poppy.

"You should come to Queen Mab's petting zoo more often, Poppy," said Sylva. "I've learned so much about animals there."

"I will . . . sometime," said Poppy. Truth be told, Poppy was a bit nervous around animals. That's why she was so happy to find this little doll kitten, curled up and still, and no bigger than the button on her jacket. "But now I do have my own little kitten. Even if she is a doll."

Don't you think that finding a tiny doll kitten in a magic dollhouse is enough excitement for one chapter? I do, which is why I'd better stop this chapter right here. (Because if I went ahead and told you the astonishing thing that was to happen to that kitten . . . I'd be worried you might faint!)

ten

"Now that we have a doll kitten," said Sylva when Poppy came over the next morning, "we need some doll fairies to go with her."

"You're right," said Poppy. "Too bad it's not summer. We'd be eating corn on the cob. And we could save the corn husks to make dolls."

"I think there might be some corn husks in the mud room," said Sylva. "Clara hangs flowers and plants there to dry. She might have saved some husks. You never know with her."

Sure enough, next to a posy of lavender

drying from the rafters, not far from the rose hips and herbs and flowers drying for pots of fairy tea, and just behind a sheaf of pussy willows, there was a bunch of corn husks.

"Perfect!" said Poppy. She carefully took down the husks and turned to her friend. "We'd better get some water from the spring to soak these in," she said. "Then we'll be able to twist them into shapes."

"This sounds pretty tricky," said Sylva. "We could just make twig-fairies instead." Sylva's craft projects sometimes didn't turn out quite the way she hoped they would.

"Tricky but worth it," said Poppy. "Let's give it a try."

"As long as you do the hard parts!" said Sylva.

"I will, I promise," said Poppy. They did their secret best-friends handshake: two shakes, a spin around, and three wing touches. "Iris showed me how to make dolls out of corn husks last summer," said Poppy.

"I think Clara showed me, too," said Sylva, "but I forgot!"

"What did I show you?" asked Clara, flying into the fairy house. She was carrying a bucket of water, which she set down without spilling a drop. She saw the sheaf of husks in Poppy's hands. "Oh! I bet you're making corn-husk fairies. May I help?"

"You already have," said Poppy. "We were just going to get some water, but now we don't need to."

It wasn't long before Iris and Susan Flower joined in, stopping on their way to plant some flowers in the queen's cutting garden.

"Fairy dolls!" said Iris.

"I loved doing this when I was just a little fairy like you two," said Susan.

"We're not little!" said Poppy and Sylva together.

Then Goldie and her best friend, Avery, showed up. Avery said she would make the dolls some clothes, and Goldie insisted on glitter for their wings. "Otherwise, they're *so* drab!" she said.

Rosy and Squeak came in from their morning stroll.

"Lolo," said Squeak in a small voice.

"Oh, Squeak, of course you're sad," said Rosy.

"There's no baby fairy!" So she and Squeakie got to work on a (very lopsided) baby fairy doll. Between twisting the stalks and tying the knots and cutting the ends to make everything look nice and even, there was a lot to do. But not one of the fairies wanted to stop, except for a quick break for cookies and rose-hip tea.

When at last all the snippets of twine and glitter and cloth had been swept away, and the corn-husk dolls were all assembled in the fairy dollhouse, Sylva, Poppy, and their sisters sat back proudly to look at their work.

"It's a fairy-doll family," said Poppy.

"Ahhma," said Squeak.

"Yes," said Sylva. "Almost like magic."

eleven

ylva and Poppy had wanted to have a sleepover that night, but Clara insisted that they needed a good night's sleep, and they could meet up again in the morning. But Sylva was restless after dinner. "I'm going for a flyabout," she told Rosy. "I'm on the lookout for feathers. We need some for the dollhouse garden."

"Would you like me to go with you?" asked Rosy. "Goldie can look after Squeak for a bit."

"Not for long, though," said Goldie.

"No, I'm fine," said Sylva. "I'll go down to

the osprey nest on the point to see what I find there."

The biggest, messiest osprey nest on Sheep-skerry Island was out near Pirates' Cove. Sylva collected fourteen feathers from underneath the nest, enough to build a feather fence all the way around the fairy dollhouse. She turned to go home.

It was a lovely mild spring evening, and Sylva was enjoying her flight. Just before she flew out of the cove, she caught a sweet gust of wind that took her up into the sky.

"Wheeeeeee!" she said. Sometimes it *was* fun to act like a little fairy and just play on the wind. Now she was high over the ground. She looked out to sea.

The water was still and calm. The air was clear. Way out in the water, far, far away from Sheepskerry, a ship loomed into view. Sylva stared at it for a minute. There was something

unusual about the ship. Something that didn't seem quite right. Then she realized what it was.

I've never seen a ship with such dirty old sails before, she thought. *They're almost black.*

Then she caught another gust of wind. "Wheeeeeeeee!" she cried, and she floated away.

I don't suppose *you* know what kind of a ship

has filthy black sails, do you?

Or what kind of sailors would be aboard such a ship?

I'll give you a hint.

Sometimes, they say, "Aaaargh."

twelve

When Poppy came over the next day, there was a lot to do in the fairy dollhouse. Now that there was a family of fairy-doll sisters, everything had to be rearranged.

Poppy moved two beds into the upstairs bedroom and put the baby in the crib in the downstairs great room, which is where all fairy babies sleep. Sylva added enough chairs around the dining room to seat all the fairy dolls. Together, they made plates out of buttons and pillows out of pussy willow buds, and soon the house looked as lively and happy as it ever could have in Queen Mab's day.

"I'm just going to dab a little paint on this old kitchen chair," said Sylva, "so it looks nice enough for our house."

"Careful, Sylva," said Poppy.

"I'm always careful," said Sylva. She took out a jar of white paint (which she had discovered in the pile under her bed). "I'll just shake this up and—"

Do you suppose Sylva had tightened the lid before she shook the paint? She had not!

Paint spattered all over the two fairies. Luckily, it missed the dollhouse almost entirely. Only the little doll kitten got some paint on her tail.

"Oh, Sylva!"

"It's not too bad!" cried Sylva. "Quick, wash her off!" Sylva splashed water on the tiny gray doll kitten, and soon her fur was pretty clean.

"Let's put her on a stone to dry in the sun," said Poppy.

"There's a sparkly one over near the rose bed," said Sylva.

Poppy carefully and gently picked up the tiny kitten and put her into the palm of her right hand. Sylva cupped her left hand over Poppy's. Together they walked slowly toward the sparkling stone.

All at once, a gust of wind came up. The trees rustled. The air swirled with blossoms. The sun came out from behind a cloud. A bright rainbow of light shone right onto the tiny doll kitten.

And at that moment, the little gray doll cat turned into a

real

live

fairy

kitten.

thirteen

Clara thought the house was on fire.

"YI-EEEEEEEEEEEEEE!"

"WHOOOOOOOOOOOW!"

"Poppy! Sylva! Are you hurt? What's going on?"

Sylva and Poppy burst into the kitchen along with one fairy kitten and a whole lot of excitement.

"She's real!"

"She came alive!"

"She got big!"

"There was a light—"

"Maybe it was Tinker Bell!"

"And then . . . she turned into a real kitten!"

The thing about magical islands is that you never know when magic is going to happen. Maybe Tink was thinking of her little sister Sylva at that very moment, and sent a charm her way. Maybe there was old magic in the air from the days of fairies long ago. Many years afterward, when Sylva told the story around the summer campfire to the younger fairies, she led them to believe that it was Queen Mab who brought the kitten to life. But to this day, no one knows for sure.

Poppy and Sylva certainly did not care how the magic had happened. All they knew was the magic did happen, and it happened to them.

"A kitten! She's a real live kitten!" Poppy cried. The fairies could not take their eyes off the darling little cat. She wasn't doll-sized anymore.

She was just as big as a real kitten ought to be.

She had gray fur, and two bright blue eyes that made her look as if she could almost understand everything you were thinking. And there was a dab of white at the end of her tail.

"I cannot believe she's a real cat, Poppy!" Sylva said. "We are so, so—"

"*Lucky!*" They both said that word together.

"Let's call her Lucky!" said Sylva.

"That's a perfect name," said Poppy. "You are Lucky, my little kitten." She tried to give Lucky a kiss, but Lucky squirmed out of her arms and darted across the kitchen floor. "I'll have to learn how to hold her better," said Poppy. "Get her, Sylva!"

"I'll show you," said Sylva. She had held so many tiny animals at the petting zoo that she knew just what to do. She scooped up Lucky with both arms and gave the squirmy kitten a big hug. "Whoa! She won't keep still. Let's get her something to eat. Can you believe we have a kitten of our very own?"

Clara took Lucky from Sylva and looked at the kitten very carefully. She had had some experience with injured animals that needed to be rescued.

"Well, she seems to be in very good shape," said Clara. Lucky cocked her head to one side as if to say, *Of course I am! I'm in great shape!*

"Can I try to hold her again," asked Poppy, "if I am very careful?"

"Cradle her—like a baby," said Clara, "and let's get her some food. She may be hungry."

Sylva opened up the pantry of the Bell sisters' kitchen. She wasn't exactly sure what to feed a kitten. One reason was that Sylva had never had a pet of her own. But another reason was that there were almost no fairy pets on Sheepskerry Island.

I'm sure that surprises you. It surprised me when I first learned of it. You'd think that Sheepskerry would be just the place to have pets galore. But other than the occasional turtle and one or two crickets, most fairy sisters had never had a pet, nor had they even thought of having a pet. Queen Mab felt it was too dangerous.

If you think about it for a moment, you can see that she *might* be right.

Fairies are very small, by our standards. They can fit in the palm of the hand of a child. Fairy pets are even smaller than fairies. And if those pets are kittens or puppies, they can be cute and adorable and funny and loving, but there's one thing they cannot do: They cannot fly.

Imagine a darkening twilight at Lupine Pond. Imagine a curious kitten in the tall grass. Imagine a great horned owl looking for its dinner.

And imagine—

Actually, I'm not going to ask you to imagine anything else.

That's why Queen Mab had a petting zoo at the palace, and the fairies took turns taking care of the animals there. She did not forbid pets on the island, but she certainly did not encourage them.

"Kittens need healthy meals," said Poppy. "That's one thing I know."

"How about some fresh fish?" asked Sylva. "We have some in the icebox."

"Fresh fish, and a little springwater," said Poppy. "That will be perfect for a baby kitten like my Lucky."

They took out a small saucer and put the springwater in that. The fish went in a little plate just next to the saucer.

"Pssst! Pssst! Here, Lucky!" said Poppy. Lucky came right over. "She does what I say!"

"I think she might just be hungry, Poppy," said Sylva. "Look at her eat that fish! This is probably the first meal she's ever had that wasn't made of pretend food."

"Imagine! You were a doll kitten all your life," said Poppy to Lucky when she had finished her food. She petted the little kitten carefully.

"Now you're going to be one curious cat, aren't you, Lucky?"

And as if Lucky had heard Poppy's words, she lifted her head, opened her eyes wide, and darted out of the kitchen.

"Oh no! She could go anywhere!"

"She's in this house somewhere. Let's find her, Poppy!"

fourteen

The two friends flew high and low and finally found Lucky playing in a huge pile of shirts and blouses up in Goldie's room. "Lucky, you are so adorable!" said Sylva. "Even if you are good at running away."

Poppy waved Goldie's red-and-white polka-dot blouse in front of Lucky. She pounced on it, batted it once or twice . . . and then she flipped! "Ooh!" cried the two friends together.

Clara called up the stairs. "Fairies! I'm heading over to the Flower sisters' for the evening. Are you two going to be all right with that kitten?"

"We'll be fine!" Sylva called back.

"You'd better get Lucky out of Goldie's room before she comes home," Clara said as she was leaving. "She'll love Lucky, but she won't love the idea of her precious clothes being used as toys. See you later! Take good care of your kitten!"

Sylva could not resist letting Lucky play in Goldie's room a little bit longer. "I'll just borrow this one shirt for Lucky to play with," she said to Poppy. "She likes it so much, and Goldie never wears it." Lucky pounced when Sylva waved the shirt. "You hold Lucky while I clean up."

Poppy looked a little worried. "I'm not so good at holding Lucky, Sylva," she said. "You saw what happened in the kitchen."

"Honestly, Poppy, if she's supposed to be our cat, you'll need to learn to hold her," said Sylva.

Poppy carefully took Lucky from Sylva's arms. "I do need to hold her—you're right, Sylva. I'll carry her over to our fairy house so she can meet her new sisters."

"She'd be better off staying here," said Sylva. "She can get comfortable with her new surroundings."

"But she's going to live with us," said Poppy, "at our house, Sylva. You can come see her and we can share her, but she's really my cat."

Sylva couldn't believe her ears. What was Poppy thinking! The dollhouse was theirs together. They had made the doll family together and decorated the rooms together. So the cat should be theirs together, especially since it was a real live fairy kitten, not just a doll. What did it matter where Lucky was when they first spotted her? She could have been anywhere, and she just happened to be upstairs. Sylva noticed that Lucky was squirming even more in Poppy's arms.

"You can't even hold Lucky properly," said Sylva. "You're doing it all wrong."

"Am not!" said Poppy.

"Are too!" said Sylva.

"She's mine and I'll do whatever I want with her," said Poppy.

"Fine!" said Sylva. "Take her to your house! It's lucky she's called Lucky, because she'll need a lot of luck with you!"

Poppy's face turned white. "I'm going home now," she said. "You can come over to see my cat anytime. But a real friend wouldn't tell me I'm not good enough to take care of her."

"Then maybe I'm not your real friend," said Sylva.

With Lucky clinging to her shoulder, Poppy flew downstairs and out the door.

"Odeo!" said Squeak.

Rosy and Squeak had come in from their afternoon walk.

"Sylva, what's going on?" asked Rosy.

Sylva burst into tears. Between gulps, she told Rosy the whole story of the paint and the rainbow light and the cat that came to life. "Poppy is going to need help with that kitten," said Sylva. "But she won't get it from me." She flew up to her room and slammed the door.

If Sylva had not done that, she might have been able to hear Rosy telling her not to take things too hard. She might even have heard Squeak saying "Ma-bo-bo" over and over again.

But Sylva heard none of these things. She only heard the sound of herself crying, as the beautiful spring day wore on.

fifteen

The next morning, Sylva didn't know who to be maddest at: Lady Courtney, for giving them the dollhouse. Poppy, for saying that Lucky was hers. Lucky, for going with Poppy! Or herself, for picking the down-stairs instead of the upstairs.

She went outside in the garden and saw the dollhouse sitting there. It didn't look so pretty anymore. Sylva sniffled.

"No lolo," said Squeak.

"I can't help being sad, Squeakie," said Sylva.

"Why don't you fly over to Poppy's and

say you're sorry?" said Rosy. "She'll forgive you. And it *would* be hard to share a kitten in two different fairy houses. I'm sure you know that."

"I would have shared, if we'd found Lucky downstairs in the dollhouse! You know I would have!" Sylva said that extra loud so she would believe it herself. But in her heart of hearts she *could* imagine that it would have been very hard to share a cat. "I suppose it would have been a little bit difficult," she added in a small voice.

"You could say that to Poppy," said Rosy, "just for starters. Then maybe things will sort themselves out."

Sylva knew that was a good idea. But then she saw the red spotted blouse. Which made her think of Lucky doing those adorable flips. Which made her think of Poppy holding Lucky. Which made her think of how Poppy had a kitten, and she didn't.

"I'm not going over to say sorry to Poppy. Poppy can come here and say sorry herself!"

Sylva spent a pretty dismal day on her own at the Bell sisters' fairy house. Rosy was busy helping Squeakie sort her shells. Goldie had been out with Avery all day, trying on their new clothes from the jumble pile. Clara had stayed for a sleepover with the Flower sisters, which made Sylva feel even more alone.

The fairy dollhouse was not much fun to play with by herself. She arranged the corn-husk dolls and tried to make up a story about their fairy-doll family. But every story she made up was sad. *Maybe I'll make a puppy out of corn husks and it will come to life!* thought Sylva. *That would really show Poppy.*

But she didn't know how to make a puppy out of corn husks. And Poppy wasn't there to show her.

"Sylva! I'm back! How's the kitty?"

Clara's bright voice raised Sylva's spirits a little. Clara was so wise; Sylva would tell Clara all about what Poppy had done to her, and then Clara would *make* Poppy share Lucky.

Clara flew into the back garden. Sylva's courage faltered a little when she saw her big sister. Clara wouldn't like to hear that Sylva and Poppy were fighting.

"Hi, Sylva. You look so unhappy! Where's Poppy? And how's the kitten?"

"Oh, I'm fine. And I guess the kitten is fine. I wouldn't know," said Sylva. "She's over at the Flower fairy house. With Poppy."

"That's right," said Clara. "I saw her there this morning. Why aren't you over there with Poppy, Sylva? She's making cat toys for Lucky."

Sylva could hardly *bear* to hear that Poppy was making toys for Lucky without her. How could she? She looked up at her big sister. "We had a fight," said Sylva in a very small voice. "And I told her that if she wouldn't share Lucky, I wouldn't be her friend."

"Oh no, Sylva! You must have been very angry at her."

Sylva's eyes filled with tears. "I was! I was so mad that she wouldn't say Lucky was ours together. I told her she'd be bad at taking care of her own cat! But now I feel terrible that I said that."

Clara looked at Sylva thoughtfully. "I'm sure you do," said Clara. "But it can't be easy for you, thinking that Lucky belongs to Poppy."

"It's not. You should go tell Poppy how bad I feel,"

said Sylva. "Then she'd be sorry. Maybe she'd listen to you."

"Maybe she would," said Clara. "But I think it's always better for two friends to work things out for themselves, don't you?"

Sylva didn't reply. "I'm going out for a fly around the island," she said, "so I can think about how unfair everything is. Plus, I want to see if that ship is still there."

"What ship?" asked Clara.

"The big one, way out on the horizon," said Sylva. "I'm sure it's gone now."

"Was it . . . a gnome boat?" asked Clara. She blushed, and Sylva knew why. Clara had a crush on one of the gnomes who'd visited last winter.

"Nope, too big," said Sylva. "And the sails were really dirty. Not like a gnome boat at all."

"You go out and clear your head," said Clara. "And if that ship is still there and if the sailors need help with their spring-cleaning, let me know."

Clara and Sylva couldn't possibly know it, but spring-cleaning was the last thing on those sailors' minds.

sixteen

I don't want you to be too shocked in the next part of the story so I think I'd better let you in on a secret. The sailors aboard that ship were not just an untidy bunch. They were a lying bunch. A thieving bunch. A very mean bunch indeed. For aboard that ship were PIRATES.

Now, please, do not be too worried. Pirates don't often sail into the waters near Sheep-skerry. And when they do, they rarely land on Sheepskerry Island. In fact, Queen Mab never seemed to worry about pirates at all. There hadn't been a pirate sighting on Sheepskerry Island for many fairy years. And there had been no signs of pirate camps on the fairy island's shores for many years longer.

But the *Bilgewater* was a pirate ship, all right. Captain Sinker was at the helm with Mr. Leakey as his mate. The captain was looking through his spyglass. He squinted, and so did Mr. Leakey. Their sights were set squarely on—

"Sheepskerry Island," said the captain with a nasty laugh. "Wouldn't you say, Mr. Leakey?"

"I would, Cap'n!" said Mr. Leakey,
who agreed with the captain as if his life depended on it, which it often did.

Captain Sinker flourished a large red handkerchief and blew his nose.

HAAAWNNK. "Ripe for the plundering. Full of the treasure I crave." He sniffed again.

"Aye, aye, captain," said Mr. Leakey. "We *all* crave treasure." Mr. Leakey often *dreamed* of treasure. "Um . . . what kind of treasure be it, Cap'n? Will there be plenty for all?"

"There'll be nothing for you unless I say there is," Captain Sinker roared. He noticed that Mr. Leakey was drooling. "Wipe yer mouth, ye gaping toad, and turn the tiller toward Sheepskerry." He looked out toward the magical island. "And I pity any pestering fairies who get in our way."

Oh, let's hope our fairies don't get in that pirate captain's way!

seventeen

Sylva flew out of the Bell sisters' fairy house and down toward Foggy Bottom, which was a funny name for a pretty place. It was always misty and cool down there, even on a clear spring day like this. Sylva thought the mist and the breeze might help her think.

When she arrived at Foggy Bottom, she was surprised to see Queen Mab sitting on a rock, looking out onto the water. Sylva didn't want to disturb her, but Queen Mab must have heard Sylva's wings fluttering, because she turned toward her and smiled.

"Sylva, dear," said Queen Mab, "what brings you here?"

"I'm so sorry, my queen," said Sylva. She kept making mistakes around Queen Mab!

"Not to worry," said Queen Mab. "I've actually been thinking about you."

Sylva could hardly believe it. "Thinking about me?" she asked.

Queen Mab patted a space on the rock next to her. Sylva sat down. "Yes," said the queen. "I've been thinking about you and Poppy, and what good friends you are. I could learn a thing or two from you."

Sylva didn't say anything, but she hung her head.

"What is it, Sylva?"

"I don't think you could learn anything from me," said Sylva. "I told Poppy I didn't want to be her friend."

Queen Mab shook her head. "Oh no," she

said. "That dollhouse—"

"It's not the dollhouse's fault!" cried Sylva.
"It's just that we found a cat—"

"A ginger cat?" asked Queen Mab.

"No, a little gray kitten. And it came to life!
And I should have said that I'd be happy to
share, but I wasn't happy to share and so I was

mean to Poppy and now I don't have a kitten *or* a best friend."

"Oh, Sylva," said Queen Mab. "Sharing can be so hard. So very hard."

The queen found Sylva's hand and squeezed it tight.

"That's what came between Nia and me. Only it wasn't a dollhouse we had to share." Queen Mab's voice was very low. But Sylva could have sworn she said, "It was Fairyland itself."

eighteen

Queen Mab didn't say a lot to Sylva about what was on her mind. She didn't have to. Sylva could tell that the dollhouse had caused trouble with the queen's friend, Nia. Sylva wondered who Nia was, and where she lived now. "You must miss each other so much," she said to Queen Mab. "Maybe you two can be friends again. Just saying hello might be a good place to start."

Sylva suddenly realized something. She could just say hello. Then she could tell her best friend that she had made a mistake and she was so, so sorry. Then Poppy and she could be friends again. Lucky could be Poppy's cat, but they could both play with her. Sylva could show Poppy how to hold her kitten. And they could fly her back and forth between their two fairy houses. It would be so much fun!

"Oh, Queen Mab, please excuse me! I've got to go!"

Sylva put on a burst of speed and zipped over to the Flower sisters' house. It made Sylva happy to see her friend's house—it was so pretty in the springtime, its roof bursting with trillium and bunchberries. Just looking at their pretty blossoms made Sylva happy.

She flew right into Poppy's house without even knocking on the door.

"Poppy! I'm back! I came to say—"

"Poppy's not here, Sylva," said Iris Flower.

"We wanted her to stay and help us mix our teas," said Daisy Flower. She put a purple flower

behind Sylva's ear. "But she said she needed to see you. She left an hour ago. Maybe more."

"I think she wanted to say sorry," said Iris. "She took Lucky with her."

"Oh no," said Sylva. "*I* wanted to say sorry!"

"Check back at your fairy house, Sylva," said Susan. "I'm sure she's there, playing with Lucky."

But when Sylva arrived at the Bell sisters' fairy house, Poppy was not there.

"Well, they can't be far," said Clara when Sylva told her what was going on. "I think I even saw Poppy heading toward Lupine Pond when I was out running errands earlier today. I didn't see Lucky with her, though."

That made Sylva worry.

"Don't fret, Sylva," said Rosy. "They're here somewhere. I'm not worried about Poppy. She's safe anywhere on the island, especially as the trolls are still hibernating. But if Lucky's not at the Flower sisters' house, or in Poppy's arms . . ."

"No! No! Don't say it!" said Sylva, thinking of all the terrible things that could happen to a tiny little kitten on a big island. "She might have fallen into the water! Or a hawk could get her. She's probably in danger right now. And it's all my fault!"

nineteen

Sylva had some very good sisters, especially when a crisis hit. They would all need to pull together to help her find Poppy and Lucky. And pull together they did.

Clara and Rosy knew where they'd find Goldie; she'd be over at the schoolhouse, where her best friend, Avery Pastel, lived. They flew straight there. Goldie and Avery were in the middle of a fashion show, but once Goldie heard what was happening, she left at once. "Don't try on anything without me!" she called to her best friend as she hurried out the door.

"What a ninny that Sylva is," Goldie said as they flew back toward the Fairy Village, "to say such a thing to sweet Poppy. I'm tempted to give her a good scolding when I see her."

By the time Clara, Rosy, and Goldie arrived back at home, Sylva was in such a sad and sorry state that Goldie gave her a hug instead. "Poppy can take care of herself," she told her sister. "And we'll find Lucky. Don't you worry."

"It's all my fault," said Sylva.

"Yes, it is," said Goldie. "But let's sort that out later."

"Sylva and Rosy—you scoot around the Fairy Village," said Clara, "and then around Lacy Meadow, to see if you can find Poppy. Goldie and I will head down to the dock and scour the west side of the island in case she's there."

"Squeak!" said Squeak.

"Oh, Squeakie, of course we didn't forget you," said Clara. "Rosy will take you in the fairy carrier, won't you, Rosy?"

"Climb aboard!" said Rosy. Clara lifted Squeakie into the carrier.

"Coomada!" said Squeak.

"Glad you like it," said Rosy.

"Let's sing our flying song," said Clara, "while we're on the wing. It will speed up our flight!" And as they lifted into the air, they sang:

We'll go flying 'round the island on the wing.
On the wing!
We'll go flying 'round the island on the wing.
On the wing!
We'll go flying 'round the island,
flying 'round the island,
We'll go flying 'round the island on the wing.

When they hit the last bright note, all five sisters felt better, even Sylva.

"We'll find them in no time," said Clara.

And then, thought Sylva, *maybe Poppy and I can be friends again.*

The search did not go well. No one in the Fairy Village had seen Poppy, although a few fairies recalled seeing a small gray kitten darting between the trees.

"I saw that cat a little earlier this morning," said Judy Jellicoe as Sylva and Rosy passed her on the boardwalk. "And then Poppy came along afterward. She doesn't seem to be very good with animals. Why don't you help her out, Sylva?"

Of course that only made Sylva feel worse.

"Don't worry," said Rosy. "They're going to be fine. I'm sure they're just around the next tree." But they were not behind the next tree. And the fog was rolling in.

By midafternoon, Sylva and Rosy and Squeak had looked all over the east side of the island for Poppy and Lucky. They were about to turn around to see if Clara and Goldie had had any luck when they heard a tiny—

Mew!

"Rosy! It's Lucky!" Sylva cried.

They saw a streak of gray fur heading down to the shoreline.

"Not that way, Lucky!" cried Sylva. "Oh, Rosy, she's headed to Pirates' Cove."

Sylva and Rosy—with Squeak on her back—followed Lucky down to the cove. Sylva wasn't sure why it made her so nervous to go there. It was something about the ship and the tattered dark sails. Before she could think too much about that, she saw the blur of beating wings out of the corner of her eye.

"Poppy!" she cried. Poppy must have spotted Lucky, too. Sylva saw her alight on a high branch of a spruce tree at the tip of Pirates' Cove. Sylva was about to call out to her again—but then her voice caught in her throat.

"Don't say a word," said Rosy.

Even through the fog, Rosy and Sylva could see the same big, dingy ship that Sylva had spotted on the horizon days before. It was much, much closer now.

But that was not the worst thing.

The worst thing was that two of the sailors from the ship—one tall, one squat—were in a rowboat, splashing noisily toward Sheepskerry. Their boat was laden with pickaxes, shovels . . . and a great big treasure chest.

"Rosy, are those—"

But Sylva didn't get to finish her question. Because through the fog came a booming voice.

"Aaaargh, me hearties. Here be treasure."

twenty

Pirates!

Rosy and Sylva looked at each other in dread. They had read about Captain Hook and his terrible pirate crew in the book called *Peter Pan*. They knew just how horrible pirates could be.

"Eee lalee!"

"Don't be scared, Squeakie," said Rosy, her voice rising just a little in fear. "We'll keep you safe from the pirates." She turned to Sylva. "Look, Sylva. I'll go warn Poppy. You take the fairy carrier off my back so I can—"

"We don't have time for that!" said Sylva.

"You're right," said Rosy. "We've got to get Squeakie out of danger now."

"You'll have to fly to the palace to tell Queen Mab what's happening," said Sylva. "And I'll take care of Poppy and Lucky."

"Be careful, Sylva!" Rosy gave Sylva a quick, fierce hug and flew off, faster than Sylva had ever seen her.

Now to keep Poppy and Lucky safe from the pirates, thought Sylva. *And me too!*

Sylva kept an eye on her best friend up in the spruce tree. Poppy must not have seen the pirates yet. Her gaze was fixed on the tall grass, where Lucky was playing hide-and-seek. Sylva flew up to her as quietly as she could.

"Poppy!" she whispered.

If Poppy hadn't been so good at balancing, she might have fallen off, such was her surprise and joy at seeing her best friend flying toward her.

"Sylva!" cried Poppy. "I'm so happy you're here!"

"Oh, Poppy, I'm so, so sorry!" said Sylva. "Can you forgive me, please?"

"Forgive you?" Poppy said. "I was the one who was wrong. Can we still be best friends?"

"Yes! Oh yes, please!" Sylva and Poppy hugged each other hard. It was so good to be friends again! "Oh, I missed you so much, Poppy!"

Then Poppy looked down from the branch. "Do you see Lucky down there?" she asked. "I would have flown down to pick her up, but those sailors coming ashore . . . they gave me a chill."

"I'm glad you didn't. Do you know what kind of sailors they are?" asked Sylva.

Poppy looked at the rowboat as it came closer and closer. She studied the two villainous-looking rowers.

"They're not—"

"Yes, they are!" said Sylva. "They're pirates. And they're here to steal treasure!"

"Oh no!" said Poppy. "And look—they're already ashore. We've got to act quickly to get Lucky out of danger. Ourselves, too!"

"Shh...," said Sylva. "Those pirates are saying something. Let's listen." *It may save us,* she thought. Both fairies sat perfectly still as they leaned in to hear the pirates.

"This fog don't please me, Mr. Leakey. It don't please me one bit," said the taller pirate as he and his mate unloaded the rowboat onto the shore of Pirates' Cove. Then he wiped his nose on his sleeve.

"Yuck," said Sylva.

"He looks like the captain," Poppy whispered.

"I don't like the fog neither, Cap'n Sinker," said his companion. "But where be the treasure?"

"One's called Sinker and the other's Leakey!" said Poppy, laughing as quietly as she could. "They can't be very good sailors!"

"Or pirates!" said Sylva. She was laughing too. "We've got to keep quiet, Poppy. Let's hear what they're saying."

"This fog be as thick as pea soup. Just like the soup me dear old ma used to make," said Captain Sinker. "And the same color, too. *WAAACHOO!*"

"What a sneeze!" said Sylva.

"Your ma warn't much of a cook, then," said Mr. Leakey.

Captain Sinker sighed. "No, she warn't." He coughed loudly. "*ACK ACK ACK!*"

"That pirate captain has a bad cold," said Sylva. "Next time he sneezes, let's scoop down and get Lucky. Then we'll fly away home!"

"Got it!" said Poppy.

"Ma is the reason I ran away to sea, bless

her," said the pirate captain. He was poking around in the grass, not too far from where Lucky played. Poppy and Sylva held their breath. "Between that soup . . . and her ghost stories." Captain Sinker shuddered. "She told me such bedtime stories about wee ghosties who came out in the fog!" He looked around at the fog rolling in on the cove. "Very much like this fog here." The captain's voice was shaking. "Ma said that thinking about ghosties would help me get to sleep."

"Nice mother," said Mr. Leakey, very quietly.

"I be ever so afraid of the wild ghosties," said the captain in a small voice. He sniffed loudly. Then he pulled himself together. "But even this fog won't keep us from seizing our treasure, Mr. Leakey," he said, rubbing his hands.

"Will there be gold for all on Sheepsferry?" asked Mr. Leakey.

"It's Sheeps*kerry*, you jackanapes," the

captain roared. He wiped his nose on his sleeve again. "And this treasure be greater than gold. *WAAAACHOOO!*"

"Let's go!"

Sylva and Poppy held hands and flew down from the tree branch. They landed right next to Lucky and picked her up together. She was not going to get away this time.

But at that very moment, as the two fairies took flight with Lucky in their arms, Captain Sinker's eyes watered. His nose itched. And he sneezed his biggest sneeze of all. "*WAAAAA-CHOOOOOO!*"

The captain reached for his sleeve and unfurled a

great

red-and-white

polka-dotted

handkerchief.

And Lucky saw him do it.

"Lucky! No! No!"

Lucky leaped out of the best friends' arms and ran straight toward the captain.

"*Mew! Mew!*"

"What's this?" cried the captain when he saw the kitten streaking toward him. "A pretty kitty for our ship?"

Lucky thought the captain wanted to play— until the captain grabbed her by the scruff of her neck and tossed her into his pirate chest.

"*Mow! Mow! Mowwww!*"

"You can stay in that trunk till we get back to the *Bilgewater*," he said to Lucky in a terrible voice. Sylva and Poppy were terrified.

"And once you be aboard, my pretty kitty, you can eat up all our rats." He laughed his nasty laugh. "Unless they eat you first." He slammed the trunk closed with Lucky inside. "It's a pirate's life for you, my pretty," he said. "A pirate's life for you."

twenty-one

Poppy and Sylva watched the scene in horror.

"What will we do?" said Poppy, near tears.

"We can't steal that treasure chest," Sylva said. "It's too heavy. And the pirates might see us, and then they'd—" Sylva did not want to say what the pirates might do to two young fairies and their pet kitten.

"*Meeew! Meeew!*" cried Lucky from inside the pirate trunk.

"Oh, she's breaking my heart!" said Poppy.

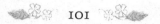

"And this fog is so spooky. It's making everything worse and—"

Sylva's eyes lit up. "What did you say?" she asked.

"I said the fog was making everything worse!"

"No, before that," said Sylva. "You said the fog was—"

"Spooky," said Poppy. And her eyes lit up, too. "I know what you're thinking!" she said. "I heard him say it too!"

They both remembered Captain Sinker's words, *I be ever so afraid of the wild ghosties.*

The two best friends looked at each other. "I'll fly out to the middle of the cove," said Sylva in a rush. "Then I'll make a sound like a ghost, and they'll be scared, so I'll swoop in and—"

"Sylva?" said Poppy. "Why don't we make a plan . . . together?"

Sylva put out her hand and Poppy smiled.

"Secret best-friends handshake!" Two shakes, a spin around, and touch wings together! Then they quickly came up with a plan.

"Do you think it will work?" asked Poppy.

"It has to!" said Sylva. "Let's go!"

Acting as one, Sylva and Poppy flew to their places. Poppy perched higher up on the spruce tree. Sylva quietly glided to a rock near the captain's shovel.

"*Wooo-oooooo!*" called Poppy in her spookiest voice.

"*Woooo-hooo-hooo!*" called Sylva, sounding even more ghostly.

"What was that?" said the captain. He tensed.

"Just the wind, Cap'n," said Mr. Leakey. "Do I dig here? Do this be the treasure?"

"*Whooo dares disturb our island?*" called Poppy.

"Did you hear that, Leakey?"

"I did, Cap'n! It be the fairies trickin' us."

"*Whoooooo steals our kitten?*" called Sylva.

"Those ain't fairies. Those be ghosts!" said Captain Sinker. "The wee ghosties who come out in the fog!"

Sylva almost laughed out loud at the pirate captain, and she was sure Poppy was doing the same. *Our plan is working!*

"*Giiiiive us baaaaaaack our kitten,*" said Sylva. "*And weeeeeeee'll haauuuuuunt you no moooooore!*"

"Do as they say, Leakey!" shouted Captain Sinker. "Give them the kitten, and let's scarper!"

"What about the treasure, Captain?" asked Mr. Leakey. "We can't leave till—"

"Let's be gone, man! I'll just grab as much treasure as I can." The captain ripped up some flowers from where Mr. Leakey was digging.

"You're picking flowers, Cap'n?"

"I have me reasons, Leakey!"

"Gooooooooooo *now!*" called Sylva. "*Leeeeeeeeave the kitten to ussssssss!*"

"*Turn awaaaaaay from the treasure chesssssst,*" called Poppy, "*so we can releeeeeease the kitten!*"

With his knees knocking and his hands shaking, Captain Sinker turned his back on the treasure chest. "Didn't you hear them, Leakey?" the captain asked. "Leave that chest and do as they say, or they'll haunt you all your life, just as Ma warned me!"

In a flash, Sylva and Poppy flew over to the treasure chest. With a huge effort, they lifted up the lid and turned the chest on its side. Lucky took one look at the two friends smiling in on her, flipped out of the chest, and seemed as pleased with herself as she could be.

"Pick her up like this, Poppy," said Sylva in a whisper, showing her how. Poppy scooped up Lucky in one sure movement and held her tight. "Now let's get out of here!"

"C-c-can we go now, ghosties?" asked Captain Sinker. "Pretty please?"

"*Awaaaaay with you now,*" said Sylva. "*And don't daaaaaaaarken our island again.*"

"Oh, thank ye, ghosties, thank ye," said Captain Sinker.

"I still think they were fairies," said Mr. Leakey.

But by that time, Captain Sinker had dragged Mr. Leakey into the rowboat, and they splashed their way back to the *Bilgewater*.

Lucky, who seemed to think it was all a game, purred in Poppy's arms.

"You did it, Sylva! You beat the pirates!"

"We did it together, Poppy," said Sylva. "Now let's go home!"

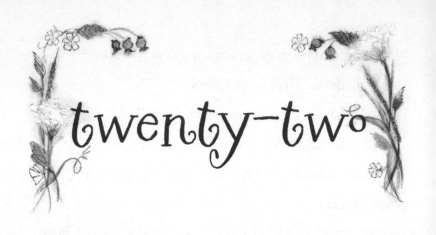

twenty-two

The next day, after Sylva and Poppy had told all their friends the story of the pirates (which got better every time they told it), they pulled out the dollhouse again.

"Poppy, let's just say the whole dollhouse is both of ours," said Sylva, smiling, "upstairs and downstairs. And Lucky is your kitten, who'll live at your house—but I'll visit all the time!"

"Are you sure that's fair?"

"Fair and square to share," said Sylva.

"We still haven't decorated the whole house," said Poppy. "Why don't we move this rug out of the bedroom into the kitchen?"

"Wait a minute," said Sylva. "What's under here? Looks like there's a crack in the floor." She carefully lifted up the rug. "That's not a crack," she said. "That's a secret door!"

Carefully, cautiously, Sylva opened the secret trapdoor. "This must be the dolls' root cellar," she said. "What's down here?"

And then she saw it. A tiny bundle of ginger fur lying in a patch of sunlight. "Oh, Poppy! It's another doll kitten."

"Another kitten!"

"Do you think it will come to life, Poppy? Like Lucky did? Or is it just a doll kitten forever?" *Didn't Queen Mab say something about a ginger cat?* Sylva thought.

"We took Lucky out into the sun," said Poppy. "Let's do that with—"

"—with Ginger," said Sylva.

They took the tiny little furry kitten into the sun. "This is exactly what we did with Lucky," said Sylva. "We were walking over toward the sparkly stone. And then there was a breeze—" Sylva's hair blew gently across her face.

"A breeze like this one!" said Poppy.

"And then a ray of light, like a rainbow," said Sylva. "And then . . ."

"*Mew!*"

Turns out Ginger was a real cat, too.

twenty-three

Sylva had never been happier. Now she had a ginger kitten of her very own. But better than that, she had her best friend.

"Let's go show Queen Mab our kittens," said Poppy later that afternoon.

"Good idea!" said Sylva.

The two friends flew to the palace with their kittens snugly in their arms. But when they arrived there, Lady Courtney told them Queen Mab was gone.

"Gone?" said Sylva. "But she never goes away, except to her summer palace."

"And it's only spring," said Poppy.

"She's gone off on very important business," said Lady Courtney. "I don't even know when she'll be back."

Sylva and Poppy were disappointed. They turned to go. But at that moment, they heard Queen Mab's trumpet sounding through the woods. They looked up to see not one queen flying toward them but two!

Queen Mab looked as elegant as ever, but her smile was even broader than usual. The other queen was dressed in robes of gorgeous purples and sparkling silver. She carried a sleek black cat in her arms.

"That must be Queen Titania!" said Sylva. "Goldie told us all about her after she went to her palace on the mainland last fall."

The two young fairies fell to their knees.

"Please, no need for that," said Queen Mab as she flew over to Sylva and Poppy. She took the hand of the regal fairy next to her. "Shall we tell them what we've been up to, Nia?"

Nia! Sylva and Poppy looked at each other, their mouths open. Did this mean *Queen Titania* was Queen Mab's best friend?

Queen Titania spoke. "Queen Mab came to see me on the mainland, and we started talking again. After all these years."

"*I* started talking again after all these years," said Queen Mab.

"I had hoped that my fancy-dress ball last year would make us friends again," said Queen Titania, "but it took you two to help us change."

Queen Mab turned to Sylva. "I remembered

what you told me on the rock yesterday, Sylva. You were right. Saying hello was a good place to start."

Sylva beamed. She was so proud to have helped the two great queens to become friends again!

"What was your quarrel about?" asked Sylva. "Were you really fighting about all of Fairyland?"

Queen Mab smiled at Queen Titania. "It's a long story," said Queen Mab. "Maybe we'll tell you someday."

"Maybe," said Queen Titania. She smiled back.

"Now, shall we go to my palace for some tea?" asked Queen Mab.

Once they were settled in Queen Mab's walled garden, with their cats playing happily, and scones and blackberry jam and cups of sweet-smelling tea set out on the table, Queen

Mab asked to hear about Sylva and Poppy's pirate adventure. "Tell me more about Captain Sinker," she said. "Did he have a stinker of a cold?"

"He did! He did!" said Poppy.

"Then I know exactly what treasure he was looking for," said Queen Mab.

"Was it a magic potion?" asked Poppy.

"Was it the Narwhal's Tusk?" asked Sylva.

"Was it a treasure map that leads to buried gold?"

"It was none of those things," said Queen Mab. "Shall we show them, Nia?"

"I think we should, Mabs."

Sylva couldn't *believe* that anyone would call their queen "Mabs."

"Then come with me, fairies, and you'll see the precious treasure."

With Sylva and Poppy close at her side, Queen Mab flew over to her herb garden. She plucked a handful of small purple flowers with big fat brown centers. "It's this," said Queen Mab.

"That's the flower Daisy gave me," said Sylva.

"Not just any flower," said Poppy. "It's echinacea!"

"Ek-in-nay-sha?" asked Sylva.

"You can call it coneflower, if you'd rather," said Poppy. Being a Flower sister, she knew all about the plants that bloomed on the island.

"Some fairies use it to make them feel better when they have a cold, don't they, Poppy?" said Queen Mab.

"Yes!" Poppy said. "Iris makes it into coneflower tea. Is that the treasure Captain Sinker was looking for, Queen Mab?"

"I believe it was, Poppy," said the queen. "He comes here every so often when he gets a cold. Usually he tries to sneak on and off the island without our noticing," she added. "I guess he didn't count on you two."

"He could have just come to the dock and asked someone for a pot of tea," said Sylva.

"Oh, but that would not have been very piratey of him," said Queen Mab, and she laughed.

Queen Titania smiled, and Lucky and Ginger chased each other around the garden.

Sylva looked halfway across the tea table, thinking how lucky she was to have such good friends. "We all found our best treasure, didn't we?" she asked.

"You mean the dollhouse?" said Queen Mab with a smile.

"No, ma'am!" said Sylva.

"The kittens?" asked Queen Titania.

"Almost," said Sylva. "But not quite."

"Oh," said Poppy. "You must mean being best friends again."

All four fairies grinned. They didn't need to say a word.

fairy secrets

Squeak's Words

Ahhma: Magic

Coomada: Love it!

Eee lalee: I'm scared.

Lolo: I'm sad.

Ma-bo-bo: I love you.

No lolo: Don't be sad.

Odeo: Oh dear!

Squeak!: Oops! or Uh-oh! or Yay! or sometimes, *Yikes!*

How to Make a Fairy Kitten Toy

Cut a piece of aluminum foil about the size of a piece of paper.

Scrunch the foil into a very tight ball, making sure no edges are left hanging out, so your cat doesn't chew on them.

Tie a long piece of yarn securely around the foil ball, and attach the string to the ceiling or a chair. Make sure the ball hangs just above the floor.

Watch your cat play!

Fairy Bell Sisters' Flying Song

We'll be fly- ing round the Is- land on the wing, on the wing! We'll be fly- ing round the Is- land on the wing, on the wing! We'll be fly- ing round the Is- land, we'll be fly- ing round the Is- land, We'll be fly- ing round the Is- land on the wing!

An excerpt from

Christmas
Fairy
Magic

The Fairy Bell Sisters

Book 6

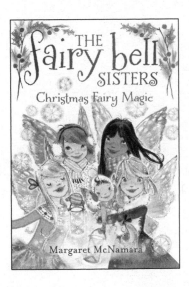

"This Christmas will be the perfect Christmas," said Goldie Bell one sparkling December morning. "I'll have so many presents!"

The Fairy Bell sisters were lying on the hearth rug before a roaring fire in the great room of their fairy house. It was a blindingly sun-filled morning, with fresh snow sparkling on every rooftop of the fairy village.

"Only ten more days till Christmas," said Sylva Bell. She was stroking a tiny kitten that was curled up in the crook of her arm. "We don't know if we can wait any longer than that, do we, Ginger?" she said. Ginger purred.

"Well, you won't have to," said Clara.

"Christmas is coming whether we'll be ready or not."

"I'm ready now," said Goldie.

"We'll be patient, won't we, Squeakie?" said Rosy Bell. She rubbed Squeak's tummy.

"O-bee!" said Squeak.

"Why not, Squeak? Why won't you be patient?" said Rosy. Squeak rolled over and rubbed her back on the side of her crib. "I don't know what's the matter with Squeak. She hasn't been at all herself lately."

"Maybe she's getting a new tooth," said Sylva.

"Or she has an upset tummy," said Clara. "Goldie, have you been giving Squeak fairy chocolates again?"

"Not too many," said Goldie.

"I'm a little worried about her," said Rosy. "Do you think—"

Just then there was a tinkling of bells

2

outside their fairy house windows. "What's that?" asked Clara. The bells had a tone that she recognized from long ago, but she did not want to risk saying what she thought. She flew over to open the door—and found no one there.

"Try the back door," said Goldie. "Maybe it's Avery. She said she'd come visit later on today."

The tinkling sound came again. Rosy looked at Clara. *Could it be?*

Sylva flew to the back door and opened it. "No one here, either," she said.

Once more the bell tinkled. Ginger scurried into the kitchen to hide. "Look! There at the window!" cried Rosy.

A dazzling beam of light filled the largest window of the fairy house great room.

"Squeak!" said Squeak.

The light was so bright and powerful that

it seemed to be knocking right on the window-pane.

Clara took Rosy's hand and squeezed it tight. "She's come back, Rosy," whispered Clara. "She's come back at last."

Meet the
Fairy Bell Sisters!